CIVILIZATION A Fight For Survival

LIFE AS IT SHOULD BE

Nitin Gupta

pencil

CONTRIBUTORS:
Versha Gupta, Aastha Gupta, Aakash Gupta, Amit Gupta, Shikha Gupta, Aayush Gupta, Akriti Gupta, Ashish Nair, Anil Gupta

ISBN 978-93-5458-375-9

Published in India 2021 by Pencil

A brand of
One Point Six Technologies Pvt. Ltd.
123, Building J2, Shram Seva Premises,
Wadala Truck Terminal, Wadala (E)
Mumbai 400037, Maharashtra, INDIA
E connect@thepencilapp.com
W www.thepencilapp.com

Author biography

The author of this book is Nitin Gupta, a resident of New Delhi India. He did schooling in Delhi and graduated in B-Tech(textiles) from Technological Institute of Textiles & Sciences, Bhiwani, Haryana.

A family man with a middle-class background, he comes from a very well to do family. Writing is his passion and it is his first book as a professional writer.

CONTENTS

Epigraph

United we stand and divided we fall

Preface

I have a knack for writing stories, fictional stories which affect our lives in the long run or in day to work. My family, wife, daughter, my son, my brother and his family too supported me a lot with ideas and making this book error-free. The compiled ideas came into being as a book that is now in your hands.

The day to day issues we deal with are all created by us humans but we never care about the issues which may crop up and threaten the very existence of ourself which, by and large, is the most intelligent being ever inhabited earth. The recent pandemic is the biggest example that has threatened the very existence of humans, it has affected us both emotionally and economically.

This book is an attempt to create awareness that we need to work on other important issues also before it gets too late.

This is my first book that got published and would be highly obliged if I get feedback both for the idea and the way of writing the book.

You can reach me at - nitingupta1972@gmail.com**or**reach my Twitter handle @nitingupta1972 for all your comments and suggestions.

Nitin Gupta

Introduction

This book tells about the present scenario of the human civilization which is very fragile in terms of our protection towards any major threat from nature. In the present society, humans are all involved in solving the problems which they have created themselves and not aware or ready for the threats they can have, which directly affects the survival of humans as a whole. This book gives an insight into how we should come together to prepare ourselves for any untoward incident which may directly affect our survival.

Chapter -1 RENDEZVOUS

It is the night of 14th Jan. 2050. Ravi was moving swiftly to his office in his car in one of the posh areas of Lutyens Delhi, it was 11.30 in the night.

He forgot some important research papers on his office desk which needs to be protected under lock and key and he has to put back into safe place anyhow as it was Friday and next 2 days office is closed.

Ravi is head of the Department Of Search On Extra-Terrestrials, ISRO. For the last 6 months, Ravi was working on a project which could be a real threat to the whole of humanity. In these 6 months, he could not sleep, eat, or concentrate anything properly.

Ravi has a family – Father, mother, wife, son, and daughter. His age is 40 years and 8 months. His family is also worried about his situation. Ravi had promised that by this month-end, he will be able to tide over this problem and discuss the detail.

Ravi reached his office and asked the guard to open the 6th floor where his research lab is. Guard, Manishanker knew Ravi very well and Ravi had been all caring with the people whom he worked and for the people who worked under him. They both went to the 6th floor through the elevator.

Manishanker and Ravi were on the 6th floor and Manishanker opened the lab and went to the reception desk leaving Ravi alone with the lab. Ravi quickly went inside and took out some files and loose papers from the computer lab desk and the high proton beam telescope base.

Taking all docs, he opened the safe vault and shelved all docs and papers in the vault only taking out a small piece of paper on which Ravi had scribbled some mathematical calculations. He quickly locked all doors again and asked the guard to lock the floor. They both then came down and then Ravi returned home with that small piece of paper.

The next day, Ravi called Rangrajun, senior project analyst to inform him about his visit to the office in the night. Ravi also asked him about the new supercomputer which was due for the department by the 17th of Jan. It was necessary to do some complicated calculations regarding his project.

On the next working day, Monday, Ravi met Rangarjun to apprise him of the total calculations of his research. By lunchtime, 1.30, in the afternoon, the new supercomputer was installed in Ravi's lab. Now, this was really great relief for Ravi to re-check his calculations.

Ravi devoted about 15-18 hrs. for the next 3 days to check

and re-check his findings. When fully satisfied and sure of his findings, he called upon the top brass of ISRO and broke the news that in the next 6 months and 21 days a fast-moving space object is on course to hit planed Earth which will destroy everything on Earth, that would be a nemesis for Earth. Now humanity has practically 6 months to save planet Earth as in 6 months it will enter into the earth's orbit which if blasted at this stage may hook off Earth from its orbit which would be more dangerous than striking the object.

In this whole scenario, the biggest mystery is that the object was unidentified as nothing similar had been ever seen in space but it was also true that it is there and moving on the collision course with Earth with tremendous speed.

ISRO, with talk to the Prime Minister, Mr. Rajmohan, and other departments of India, informed other space agencies on this issue. It was 25th Jan. 2050 and a meeting was organized with other nations' heads with their respective space agencies in total secrecy so that there is no panic among the people. At the meeting, it was cleared that this object is been traced by NASA and EPA for about a year but were very apprehensive about their findings but with this meeting and Ravi's calculation made it more comprehensive and hence the conclusion was reached to make this object nonfeasible within 4 months so to save our home.

It was April 2050, preparations were in full swing for making a laser beam to destroy the Object on its trajectory itself but there was a certain mystery about the speed of the Object. As it was approaching near to Earth, in general behaviour the speed of the Object should increase but it was getting somewhat slower. This was puzzling a lot of scientists across the world and also a thing to worry about.

On May 10th, 2050, the world was ready with its laser, with the most powerful burst ever controlled by humankind. It was decided that on 12th May, in the morning at 6 O'clock the laser will be shot at the Object. All the work, flights, and everything we're asked to be stopped to avoid any adverse effect.

The laser was shot at the Object right at the prescribed time. The laser hit hard at the Object, BUT……… nothing happened, the Object reduced the speed on its course towards the Earth. The experiment to save mother Earth failed tremendously and now we had no time to re-think our strategy and even had no plan B to tackle this situation.

Now there was panic among the stakeholders, politicians, and scientists about this danger which was fast-moving to destroy our planet. There were 2 issues with the present problem, first how to stop this collision and second is how to tell the general public about this danger.

Chapter -2 DISCOVERY

The space scientists and all the space agencies worked closely to study the Object for its structures and composition that where they failed in their first attempt. The laser was so strong that it could have knocked out a whole Earth-like planet from its trajectory.

Ravi in his lab was also working tirelessly on this Object problem. As per the Object's new speed and calculations, it was another 4 months 20 days before its rendezvous with Earth. On 20th May, at about 10.00 in the night, while Ravi was looking at the Object very closely through his meta telescope, he got a hunch that it may not be a natural Object but some kind of an unnatural Object or might be an alien ship, the thought of this created shudders in Ravi that Earth might be attacked by an intelligent alien force. He frantically jotted down his readings related to speed, structure, and momentum of the Object and sent his all observations to NASA in the US of A.

The findings from Ravi with the calculation-based theory created havoc in the US organization, A very urgent high-level meeting was called to discuss this issue. A very deep study and high-level search lead to the conclusion that as per the Object behaviour, it is endorsed world over that the Object is really an alien spaceship. Now it has to be seen that if it is empty or someone is there onboard.

A lot of preparation was done to welcome Earth's unknown guest and simultaneously preparing the world's largest army for plan B.

The announcement by various nations was made across national channels to apprise the new situation world is now facing. Some people found it an opportunity to learn about new people, their culture, and technology but some people believed that aliens are another word of destruction, they not only created false fear but also lead to far-reaching adverse in terms of social unrest.

Heads of the states requested all to remain calm and let humanity prepare for the face-off with an alien civilization that may take mankind to a new level.

By May-end, the Object stopped and hovered around the orbit of the earth without further descending. This made the scientists all across the world infer that it is an alien ship but so large that 100 football fields can be adjusted in the same.
The ship remained there and was hovering at double the speed of the earth's rotation, scientists on earth calculated that the Object crosses any earth point 2 times a day.

Now all were waiting that some smaller ships will bring the travellers to earth but nothing happened. Slowly the time was passing and with each passing day, people on earth were worried about the future course of action from the alien forces.

It is the time in which people on earth were getting time to prepare mentally and physically for any onslaught or adverse scenario from the alien forces. The other issues were how to convey ourselves to the aliens so that the 2 intelligent civilizations not only able to avoid any war and able to help each other in future also.

Chapter -3 FIRST WAVE

It was mid-June, time for a very humid climate but the climate was cooler than it should be at this point of time. Weathermen were also confused due to sudden changes in the earth's climate.

Dr Watson from ECMWF, the European Union weather agency, was studying different weather patterns in Asia and Europe and found that the weather is changing drastically and is moving ahead of time. It means that the weather which should be in September is showing now in June, it is of grave concern as humans can adapt to the changes easily but the earth's flora & fauna may not be able to adapt and may die making the earth desolate.

The cyclones and storms were now regular features, they increased about 3 folds and also the intensity was high going 180 km/hr to 220 km/hr as the wind speeds. From the satellites, one can see that most of the oceans are becoming turbulent which not only affected the sea trade but also a lot of lands came underwater.

EU and a number of weather agencies all over the world shared their concerns and agreed that this is a dangerous phenomenon. The weather agencies and space agencies came together to discuss this issue.

In 10 days' time, the conclusion was drawn that the time of changes in climate coincides with the Object entering earth's orbit, there was no definite proof of this but they all were trying to connect the dots.

It was August 2050, the Object was still flying around the earth and the weather on earth was also changing very fast, even the storms were getting with more and more strength. By October end the climate cooled down to very low temperature, the average temperature was down by almost 10 degrees Celsius all across the globe, which means the earth is entering into an ice age.

There were a lot of ice storms and floods all across the globe. A lot of vegetation died off and also affected a lot of domesticated animals. This leads to a chaotic situation all across the globe. The glaciers increased by about 40-45% making life hell in some of the most pleasant places on earth.

Every big river on the plains was flooded with water as the water from oceans were entering into the river basins, this lead to a lot of destructions in plains and these were also getting frequent and more fierce.

Some religious sects declared that doom is in near future. The climate turned topsy-turvy both with respect to strength and frequency. By this time it was established that the changes on earth's surface were due to alien ship.

This was just the tip of the iceberg, humankind was not

aware of the changes going in the earth's crust and the magnetic field which can make the planet lifeless.

In a very short span of time, say 4 months, 85% of earth was covered with ice and water due to which about 90% of the vegetation and life got extinct, it was the time of survival of the fittest.

By March 2051, the human population shrank to merely 3 billion populations from 5 billion in Jan. 2050. Now, this was the question of survival for the human race with some important plant species as food for humans. This was a fight, which was looking as never-ending with humans at the mercy of the alien species. The top forces and intellect of this planet were busy only with survival and have no time or intellect to counter these attacks.

March 2051 was the time when the earth started shaking and earth borne the most severe of the earthquakes ever seen or felt in human history. The frequency was such that each week earth shook at least 2 times with a strength of 9-10 on the Richter scale, a shock that can deliver a devastating blow to any structure how strong ever it is made. The old monuments and buildings were razed to the ground like a stack of cards, the homes were now constructed of wood or some soft raw materials to minimize damage to life and livelihoods. Due to change in magnetic fields, the communication setup worldwide got destroyed, now humans were living in groups rather than as a country or even a state as there were no facilities for long-distance calling.

This damage happened in just one and a half year after the emergence of the alien ship. Slowly and steadily, humans were losing this war without giving a fight as they have no option to counter the fury of natural changes occurring, either on their own or aliens were the reason for this havoc. In any of the ways, the earth's changes were getting uncontrollable day by day. Humankind was not able to earmark its enemy.

Chapter -4 FINAL ASSAULT

In July 2051, somehow, scientists all around the world got in contact with each other and organized a meeting and came together so to not to let the defeat creep into humans without giving a proper fight. It was decided that the enemy ship will be taken head-on in space. The planning started but due to heavy damages to the technical buildings and the death of a lot of experts made this task herculean.

Still, they started preparing a small ship to encounter the enormous ship, the ship from earth was to have the latest weaponry and most modern robots to combat aliens. The satellites which were still roaming earth gave some inputs about the space ship designs etc. Till this time nothing was known about the aliens, only the spaceship is seen and the havoc which is created on Earth.

Now it was also a big question that if the spaceship is empty and it is only creating these weather changes or some species are there in the ship which is controlling all these things. This was also creating a lot of confusion on earth that if they have to fight a war of survival against the natural forces or they have to prepare for some physical attack also.

The plan was to set up the most advanced tactical space module to combat the alien ship and was planned for September 2051 launch, which means the launch was 3 months away, this was created considering that there is alien life aboard the ship.

The planning was in full swing but we were not aware that a huge problem is awaiting for the life as a whole on earth.

In technical language, it was the third wave of attack by alien forces. It was a biological attack, a type of virus, or something else as it only has single strand protein but can travel far and wide infecting all type of living things be it humans, animals, plants, single-cell organisms, bacteria, and even virus present on earth.

This weapon of aliens was destroying life at a speed much faster than the earlier two attacks in which earth's natural resources were compromised. By September 2051, the time of launching the combat ship from the earth, the population of earth fell below 1.5 billion with 2-3 species of plants and no other fauna. All the plans were left for good, the humans accepted their defeat in just below 2 years of 1 sided war. This was the most disheartening scenario that the most intelligent and advanced civilization on earth's history was defeated without giving any fight and was on the verge of oblivion.

Now the remaining humans were waiting for the last assault which might be the combat soldiers of the alien forces coming physically on earth after making the planet lifeless and as remaining people had no capacity to fight with these forces neither technologically nor have the strength to face alien's physical onslaught.

The time came around December 2051 when the alien forces came down heavily on earth physically in their cubicle ships for the final assault.

They easily got spread all across the globe killing all retaliations and capturing the people like animals. This was the fourth wave of the attack that led to the slavery of earth to the alien forces without any fight given by the most advanced species of the earth.

This was the lesson learned by the humans all around the world that united we stand and divided we fall. Instead of making boundaries for humans and fighting with each other, they should have made the earth, human's home planet, one planet for all humans. They should have united to combat problems like disease, floods, pollution, alien attacks, etc but now it was too late, humans had already lost their home, mother earth.

Now as the earth got defeated, humans were captured to work in their convertibles, these were the production houses, which were making earth's resources useful for an alien civilization. It was now known that they came to earth in search of abundant water supplies, which was their lifeline also, they called themselves URS.

In March 2053, the large space ship in earth's orbit descended and landed on earth with a lot of alien population on board, looked as if a whole planet has shifted and were looking for a new home.

This looked that they are here for good and the earth will not be the same as we used to see. The aliens on the earth started a new type of world order in which they want to live in harmony with the earth civilization.

Chapter -5 THE CIVILIZATION

The danger which was studied in India about three years back is now seen as reality in the form of a new civilization and new world order.

New species, URS, spread all over the world and started harnessing all-natural resources as per their requirement. The human population was now less than 1 billion and 3-4 plant species were left which were original of the earth.

For the next 2 years, by the year 2055, the armed units of the URS controlled everything, and humans were helping them to harness the natural resources of the earth as per URS requirements as they were new to this planet. The earth's original inhabitants had no other option but to live with the new species which was far more strong and intelligent.

Our scientists, doctors, and other resourceful people had to help aliens to settle on the planet but were also allowed to work for the welfare of human civilization but the URS also worked with these people tirelessly so to establish themselves more smoothly

The damage caused on earth was rectified at a very fast pace as technological advances of URS and earth's technical people work together in unison. Everything was getting on the normal course so the people now becoming more conversant with each other societies.

In a matter of just 2 years, by 2057, the earth came back into its original landscape minus a lot of life which was lost forever. More and more advances were made to rectify the losses as quickly as possible. A single order was maintained without any boundaries of nations or states etc. The air became cleaner and healthier. Even humans saw the new civilization setup by the alien forces as a fully developed society.

By the end of the year 2058, humans and URS learnt to live harmoniously without disturbing each other's way of working. Now it was 2 societies of 2 intelligent beings living all over the globe together under a single rulebook, which guarantees equal opportunities for all.

Now for the last 3 years, the humans and URS were living together in harmony but they never discussed their pain with each other to date, it was still seen as a threat to each other to discuss the hostilities with each other. It is seen now that both the species had forgotten their pain. Destiny was something else, which they both were ignorant of.

Both sides worked together to make a better place to live. URS settled and worked hard as if this was their home planet although it was just 10 years since they settled properly on earth, this was the year 2064.

Slowly and steadily, both these intelligent species worked

together and did tremendous development in the field of science and technology in all physical, chemical and biological spheres. Now there was less suffering from diseases, enough food with clean water and atmosphere, which not only increased the quality of life but also, increased the standard of living for all.

The heads of the URS remain worried even after assurance from humans that they have now learnt how to live a prosperous life and they never want them to leave this planet, but according to them, they were worried about something else which they were reluctant to disclose to humans. It looked that they were worried more for humans rather than from humans.

The two intelligent species on earth were now on the path of prosperity and were working with each other closely to get things on track. This was a new system created in which now there were no caste, religion, region, colour, etc mattered but these were the early days as so there was division in the society based on the species. Under pressure or some miscreants tried to divide the society but now the basic core of life was understood by both species so it was quickly bought under control. The newborns and young children in schools were easily adapting with their new friends.

A time came when people from both, URS and humans, celebrated their happiness and mourn their sadness together. The gap in life expectancy between both the species was also very large, human's 2 generations were equivalent to URS's one generation which also helped humans in a way.

There was a regular fear among both the species that there can be a war between the 2 intelligent species as this is the law of nature that 2 developed/intelligent species cannot live in the same place. The present scenario was defying this law. Still, both were careful not to hurt each other sentiments, lesser the chance of the conflict.

Chapter - 6 The URS

By the year 2065, gradually URS started sharing their story with humans to become more open and friendly, it is said that 2 friends should not hide their secrets from each other.

The URS were from a far-fetched galaxy by the name of SUPHERA MODERA about 13.5 billion light-years from Earth, this is the same place, which is known as GN-z11 galaxy and considered the oldest and largest galaxy known to humans.

SUPHRA MODERA had about 2000 habitable star systems in which there are about 3000 planets with life. 300 planets are there which had intelligent life and capable of travelling in space light year speeds, means highly advanced civilizations that is why on planets there are no countries but whole planet work as a unit for its development and prosperity. Each planet has its own unique life forms, different from each other but each respected the other's individuality.

The star system had developed a very unique system to live in harmony. They had also faced a lot of issues in the very early days of their development but slowly they learnt that peace and harmony are the 2 basic principles of life through which they can prosper and develop their civilization.

At their star system also, they had various divisions based on the various traits within their species, accordingly, they have also divided their planet but it leads to a lot of friction within their own communities. WIn due course, they were visited by many other species which were intelligent enough to roam their galaxy. These new life forms not only tried to rule them but wanted to take all their resources to their own planets. The infighting at URS planet left no choice but to work for these intelligent species.

In due course, people at URS came together and started to work for their own good and in due course, the new life forms started giving respect to the individuality of URS, now, instead of exploiting URS, started working with URS for the betterment of all.

This lead URS to believe in themselves and they learnt the importance of unity rather than division in society. Together they not only able to defeat their enemies but they started developing their own species. They together fought diseases, disasters, attacks etc. They not only developed their own planet but were now having the knowledge to travel in their own galaxy, learning more things and establishing contacts with more civilizations.

They started developing a lot of business and cultural exchange with other intelligent civilizations in their galaxy. They form a consortium of 300 such planets which worked together to develop themselves and help in developing others also. There were a lot of primitive planets also which needed much more support to develop. Their consortium not only provided them with needed support but try to give them the knowledge they have gathered in the course of time.

Now their galaxy was like a big family in which everybody worked for each other development without disturbing each others independence or integrity. Everything was going fine till a wave of highly intelligent but barbarian species attacked their galaxy.

Chapter -7 NEMESIS

About 1000 sol years back a very high intellect civilization entered in URS galaxy cluster and started attacking different planets, starting from primitive forms of life. The intellectual species, like URS, didn't bother too much as they were not affected. This was the major fault as this gave the attacking species think that they can individually break the civilizations. They called themselves ZIGONS.

Slowly but surely they started attacking the intelligent civilizations also and propagating that they are the sole creators of life in the universe and now want to establish new forms of life under their GENESIS program. We as a civilization for 300 planets took a delegation to them explaining that we have all the right to live and prosper, they can start their GENESIS program on inhabitable planets so that more planets can become livable and also offered help if they require any. Even we contested that the creator never destroys its creation but try to make it better but they were not ready for any discussion, they just wanted to clean up all planets from life for their monstrous motto.

In about 200 sol years after ZIGONS came to SUPHERA MODERA galaxy, they started a full-fledged war with the 300 planets consortium. In another 100 sol years, half of the planets were made lifeless, either these species perished or ran whatever they got hold of like space ships and some equipment to settle on some other planet in a far-fetched galaxy. Since then the URS's ship was travelling to find a good home.

ZIGONS were barbaric in the fight and used to destroy the complete planet including life and natural resources to establish their base for some technological research. They were so advance that none of the planets in the suphera modera was able to resist the advances of the zigons.

Now, the suphera modera had no option other than work for the zigons as slaves or run away to faraway places to re-establish their civilization. URS were one of the best breeds in terms of advancement so they escaped their home planet in search of a new home. This escape was also very difficult and had to fight a fierce battle with the zigons but was somehow able to escape in the vast universe to find their new home taking with them the best minds and warriors of their planet.

Initially, they tried to find a place in their own galaxy but in about all places the zigons had maintained their base and URS do not want to engage with them in any way as they had already lost a lot fighting them.

Some planets they found absolutely empty in the suphera modera galaxy but were not suitable for their breed to create it their home planet.

Some of URS friends also escaped their respective planets

and decided to form a unified society on a new planet. This all happened in about 300 sol years. The story they told to people of the Earth was a history of 700 sol years from the present day. Roaming around the universe, URS had passed about 15 generations on their spaceship. At one point in time, URS thought that they have to establish their civilization as space wanderers and even started preparing to develop technologies and spaceships which can help them to remain afloat in space. The time has come for URS to re-establish themselves furthermore not wasting time in finding new places.

Chapter 8 The Quest

Roaming around the universe, URS had passed through several galaxies and their planets. They learnt a lot of things about the universe that they were not able to see or learn when living in the comfort zone of their galaxy and planet. They learnt new technologies and new natural laws on which the universe work.

While travelling, they came to know about the beautiful galaxy clusters, the star clouds which were the factories where stars were created with their systems. They shared the whole experience with humans about their vast knowledge and experience of this universe.

In an early exploration of URS, they entered into the galaxy system called LUMINOS where life was totally different and its formation was absolutely different as per the URS knowledge about life. Life, as known to URS and humans were the basic structure of organic material but in the luminos system, it was based on inorganic forms and that too highly intellect. Due to a lot of inorganic structures, life forms were also very different. So this was the first experience of URS in which they found a lot of different intelligent life forms living together harmoniously.

They discovered primitive life forms in the galaxy known as LAMBOS, about 20,000 light-years from our Milky Way. The life forms there were merely single-celled animals and multicellular plants. The plants were capable of protecting the planet from any untoward incidents and were considered intelligent as per the definition of intelligence of URS.

Moving further away from Milky Way, about 30,000 light-years, they found huge clusters of black holes, which means the place had seen a lot of supernovas in its history. URS experienced a huge gravitational pull near this place. They even sent a small capsule without any person aboard to a nearby dark planet. They wanted to study the effect of a number of black holes on the planets.

about 15 generations on their spaceship. At one point in time, URS thought that they have to establish their civilization as space wanderers and even started preparing to develop technologies and spaceships which can help them to remain afloat in space. The time has come for URS to re-establish themselves furthermore not wasting time in finding new places.

In a region called ALTAR, URS felt the presence of multiverse, which means the presence of the multi-universe. They investigated it further and finally, they established that there are multiple universes. Now, this was a breakthrough sort of thing as they had some knowledge on the same but now they can see it and feel the presence of the multiple universes.

These lead to the discovery of the never before seen worlds with new knowledge of physical, chemical and biological worlds. Due to this knowledge, URS were able to solve some of the age-old problems of their species. Slowly and steadily they moved further into the universe.

Then about 400 sol years back, they entered into the Virgo Supercluster area of our universe(they have already discovered the multi universes). Milky Way is also part of the Virgo Supercluster.

While travelling through this cluster, URS came across a number of civilizations like them but no civilization was ready to share their world with them. At that point in time, URS decided to fight for their survival on a planet rather than doing peaceful negotiations.

They visited more planets in the cluster with primitive civilizations or the planets which were desolate but all were not able to support their civilisation for more than a few years due to limited natural resources. Now, they have to move again for re-establishment.

URS established part of their civilisation such that it didn't put pressure on the available natural resources of the planet and the balance population moved further in search of more places. In this way, URS established life on a number of planets but remain in contact with them throughout their journey. These were blessings in disguise for the planets which were established by URS.

Chapter - 9 The Earth

About 300 sol years back, they entered in Milky Way but most of the star systems were inhabitable. URS travelled deep into the galaxy again establishing more planets and moving on with their balance people. They further moved to explore the galaxy. As per URS, they were still in contact with other civilizations which ran away from the onslaught on their consortium. The URS established on other planets were learning to recycle the natural resources, in this way self-sustaining the planet. These people also develop the systems to explore more nearby planets and learnt to use them for their own need.

Moving deeper into the Milky way, they got into a star system of 8 planets which looked desolate but a planet looked absolutely blue from the outer realms of the star system, after deep study it became clear that the planet has enough water in liquid form, this was the EARTH. URS moved here very fast but saw a large number of flora and fauna on this planet with primitive intellect species also known as humans. They studied and found that this is the best planet for their survival and growth and wanted to live in harmony with the original inhabitants of the planet but again they were in a dilemma if humans will accept their presence on Earth.

Humans gained a lot of knowledge to sustain and grow the planet as per their requirements but were now confused why a civilization which borne the onslaught of other advanced civilization did the same thing on earth's civilization.

People of earth questioned URS why they destroyed earth when they faced such an onslaught themselves, they should understand the feeling of the earthlings.

URS explained to them that they have studied the culture of Earth and found that the decision of this planet is not taken by a common system but the whole planet is divided at each level like countries, then states etc. Humans were further disintegrated into a number of sects that were always fighting for trivial things.

Different countries have different heads who take decisions not as per the good of the planet but as per their own benefits, so in such a scenario it was very tough for URS to call on a particular system with whom they can discuss their problem and reach to a conclusion. URS were themselves confused about how to start negotiations with the people on earth.

Then the answer was straight and quite obvious, they had to forcefully take over the planet. So they started with stirring the natural resources of the earth, the alien forces which are looking for space for themselves and do not know a thing about the life on the planets, have to use the force to first establish themselves without much resistance otherwise most of the time will go into wars etc. URS told them they are star travellers and had seen thousands of civilization, from primitive to much higher intellectual beings but they all have the same format of working that if a species tries to establish on a planet, tries its best to not to involve much in war with the original inhabitants, use the technology first to stir the planet's natural environment if the planet in question, able to bear these changes and remain strong then the travellers decide if they move on to some other place or try some more tough fighting arrangements. Non-violent species or highly advanced species will leave such planets and move on to other places as direct conflict can be dangerous for them also. URS stirred earth very badly and they were observing humans, they were really sad that due to them the original inhabitants were facing a lot of problems.

A fact is that URS tried its best to reduce the damage of life as much as possible. They also contested that they never used undue forces on the inhabitants, if no resistance then no attack. In a very quick session, they allowed and even helped humans to grow.

The viral wave was most devastating as the loss of life was highest in that attack. URS told that they came to know about the planned human's retaliation so to stop the losses of their people, URS had to attack with the biological weapon. This was the most dreadful attack and gave much-needed support to the armed insurgency on earth. This leads to the culmination of the war abruptly also URS started the development of the planet as soon as they established themselves on earth.

Chapter - 10 The Great Advance

As per the present scenario, they are helping the earth to regrow and are in the full process to establish original flora and fauna on earth. URS had made advances such that the health issues, pollution issues, weather uncertainties are all taken care of in a very methodological manner. This is the GENESIS of the earth by URS. Now it was no longer a problem for anybody to have basic needs to live. Everyone used to get their due share.

Most of the diseases and health issues were taken care of, the life expectancy of humans also increase by more than 100 years due to better health facilities, clean air and water and other basic needs.

Educating the young ones were on the topmost priorities for both the species, for humans it was never before experienced. In all fields of life like science & technology, governance, education was best and available to all.

URS were even helping humans to start their civilizations on other heavenly bodies of the solar system like planets and natural satellites. In the year 2075, they first launched a complete program to establish life on the moon, a natural satellite of earth, under a space organization named Space Administration Of Earth (SAE). Under this organization, it took 10 years to make living bases on about 15 heavenly bodies within the solar system. This not only provided more space to live but an abundance of natural resources. This also provided URS and humans with a base in the solar system's outer reaches to see any natural or aliens attack danger to the earth. If any such situation, then the earth can have a lot of time to save itself.

The space organization was planning that in the next 10 years, by 2095, they want to expand their civilized horizon to the most outer part of the Milky Way galaxy and URS had already scanned about 90% of MILKY way while travelling to find a home for themselves. They found a lot of primitive life forms, which were either similar to humans or less than human as far as technology and intellect is concerned. The program didn't include the habitable planets as now URS were not seeking space for their own survival but now they are expanding their civilization in unison with humans. So now they were looking for the planets, which had no life but can support life so that URS and humans could also expand their civilization to other planets.

URS also established contacts with their own people living far and wide so they can learn from each other and develop themselves accordingly. URS also established contact with civilizations friendly in Suphera Modera, so they can also help them to establish if required. These contacts with other civilizations of suphera further increased the knowledge of both URS & Humans about the universe.

Various natural satellites were developed for specialised works like medical inventions, defence research, food development and discoveries of food that were not only nutritious but can be easily grown in abundance.

Natural Satellites were established as leisure homes where people can go and enjoy all forms of entertainment. a lot of entertainment options were present, both indoors and outdoors, hills and sea beaches, sports complexes and leisure parks, from movies to clubs and casinos, all entertainment on one planet, number of such satellites were developed, near to every planet of the solar system.

Planets were developed where higher education facilities were present in abundance with proper facilities for research and development for students. All facilities related to study were available at one place itself, this not only helped in cutting the cost of travelling but gave more chance to students to interact with each other which lead to more understanding of the subjects. All species studied together irrespective of their species.

The development of specialised planets not only enhanced the experience but also helped each other to come close, understand each other better. Now the society was so interwoven that all were involved in each other celebrations or bad times.

By the year 3015, this new mixed-race civilization expanded its footprints in the far reaches of the Milky Way. They went far inside the galaxy to search and establish more contacts with other civilizations both for knowledge and strategic reasons. They went to the places which were earlier not explored by either URS or by their friend's from the suphera. The more they explored, the more they got to see new celestial phenomenons. They came across glowing stars rotating across each other giving a very beautiful view if watched in a spaceship.

They came across the planets with new kind of plant species which were not only unique but had both medicinal and physical properties. The physical properties of plants were unique in the sense that life forms are known to have biological and chemical properties only.

Great strides were made in the field of the development of natural resources which are considered as limited and non-replenishable. This not only solved the problem of scarcity but secured the future of generations to come.

Everything was going in a perfect manner and the new civilization was solving all problems, making themselves self-sufficient also this new civilization was named MISOMS. Nobody had thought that destiny is something else on which the survival of the MISOMS is at stake.

Chapter - 11 The Zigons

By 3050, in just 100 years from the URS coming to earth, a message came to the control centre of SAE on planet Jupiter, it is passed on to earth's SAE control centre. The message created a flutter among the URS scientists. When humans asked the reason for the same, they got the shock of their life. The message indicated the flashes of light seen from the centre of the Milky Way galaxy, which is about 25000 light-years from our solar system. The flashes of light were not natural, this may be indicating the presence of ZIGONS in the Milky Way. ZIGONS, the alien species, created havoc in SUPHRA MODERA. Now, this is a shock for humans and a disturbing fact for URS. This would be the second time in 100 years in earth's history that humans are on the verge of facing another destructive era, which would not be definitely as friendly as URS.

Collectively a meeting was organised between the top leaders, scientists and explorers to know the facts and to take stock of the actual situation. The present civilization has expanded its footprints as far as 10,000 lights years in the galaxy and each one has to be protected from any eventuality. This would be a herculean task.

All the base stations across the galaxy are alerted to seek any sign of danger approaching from the outer reaches of the galaxy. A complete plan was required to counter any attack at any of the base of the present civilization. Nobody wanted a repeat of what they have seen, humans saw the devastation from URS and URS have seen the same from Zigons earlier.

It was decided that they will leave no stone unturned to protect their identity now and will either win this war or perish forever. Now the plan is into working on how to handle this situation. It is now a very vast area to protect, no place can be left unprotected from Zigons.

As per the info, Zigons are about 25,000 light-years away from the solar system but about 15,000 light-years away from the last post of the MISOMS. As per the present speed, zigons can reach the misoms first post not before 60 sol years so technically misoms had enough time to prepare themselves for a full-fledged war with zigons. The preparation for this had to start now otherwise misoms can lose the precious time they had in hand due to very early warning.

It is also felt that the signal might be of something else, similar to zigons or zigons are present in the galaxy but they had no clue of misoms and they may actually be not coming for them but just roaming around the galaxy. But these conclusions are just wishes and not the fact so, at any cost, misoms had to prepare themselves to take the advantage of early warning.

The plan was made to equip each and every station with the latest scientific equipment and equip even the smallest station with all the latest weapons. The command centre was planned to overview each and every station for the preparations and movement of forces if there is war.

The misoms know how an advanced civilization attacks another civilization, their tactics and weapons. The misoms readied their plan which constituted the control of natural resources so that any attack by zigons by stirring the natural resources is rendered useless and balance is maintained on all the bases. This will not only defeat zigons in their first and fiercest attack but will give an edge to the misoms during the arms conflict. The preparations are going in full swing.

The misoms started preparing combat fleets and increased from the present 1000 units to 20,000 units to cover all possible attack zones. A regular check is kept on the movement and frequency of the flashes observed simultaneously, space surveillance also increased all across the feasible regions of the galaxy.

The frequency of flashes are increasing, the message received at the control centre of SAE kept misoms on nervous mode, but they maintain calm and increased their pace in preparing for war. Mission sorties are increased all-time high. Even the trainees are trained in the battlefield environment by conducting mock drills, they are just like real scenario.

Places of importance are protected by the laser screens on which there is no effect of any weapon attack. Main centres, natural satellites and planets are being covered under a camouflage system which is developed in recent times to avoid their detection by enemies.

Misoms are determined to win this war and finish zigons forever as this is the only way out for misoms survival.

It is now a matter of time when two forces will fight for their supremacy. Will misoms able to destroy zigons? What would be the result of the expected war? Why Zigons want supremacy in the universe? Is there something stored for Zigons & Misoms to learn for the war?

This all is coming shortly.

List of Contributors

A lot of people contributed to my first book, I thank all below from the bottom of my heart and thank those also who influenced me to write this book knowingly or unknowingly.

Notes

1. Rendezvous

This is the situation when humans were on the brink of meeting aliens. This is the fact that instead of the excitement of meeting a new breed, we are afraid of their attack. This is somewhat true also as all the living beings are first concerned about their safety.

2. Discovery

This is the most important aspect of human society. Human civilization never foresees the issues they can face due to their actions but take on the problems head-on as and when it comes which sometimes backfire.

3. First Wave

Human civilization has hampered natural resources so much that a small change in weather can create havoc on earth. This change can come from any outside attack or from the environmental effects on earth. The exploitation of earth resources will not only disturb the balance on earth but will get depleted in due course leaving nothing for our future generations.

4. Final Assault

The disease is the worst enemy of human civilization and in recent times we have seen that the most powerful economies of the world felt helpless against highly infectious disease. Humans can survive a holocaust but are helpless against the disease as it not only affects the health but destroys the economy also.

5. The Civilization

Human civilization achieved what no other species on earth ever able to achieve, this makes us humans more responsible for keeping our natural surroundings and resources intact. We should pass earth as we got it from our ancestors, this is not only our responsibility but it is right of our future generations. The only secret of civilization to prosper is peaceful co-existence and this is the need of our times.

6. The URS

The peaceful co-existence should not only be within the own species but it is also necessary to co-exist with other species around you to live peacefully, lest it would be effect your own existence.

7. The Nemesis

The threat can come from anywhere so we should be prepared for any eventuality, natural or self-inflicted. Peaceful co-existence will not only reduce the self-inflicted disasters but also help in overcoming any natural threat. The threat of survival from anybody should be a contest by one and all, it may or may not affect your survival directly but keeping mum on such matters not only show your acceptance towards the threat towards others but when you get the similar threat, you may also face the non-cooperation from others.

8. The Quest

The survival and development of civilization depend on how keen the people are on learning new things. People can work towards prosperity by regularly indulging in something new, it can be either socially, economically or technologically. Development in social structure is most important as it removes social evils and brings the generations and people together.

9. The Earth

Our home planets and the most beautiful planet of our solar system which harbours a number of life forms in all sea, earth and air. This is our home where we get everything to live from nature for which we have to pay nothing and still we don't care for the same. We are not using these resources but exploiting them for our lust. Our planet has enough for all if we use it but we exploit these resources and hence we are not only destroying our surroundings but making it useless for future generations. People are working to find new places in the solar system to just save humans in the eventuality that the earth is rendered lifeless but we cannot put our entry to save it so that new places are not required for resettlement but used for human civilization expansion.

10. The Great Advance

Advancement in civilization is the basic structure of intelligent life which helps it to evolve. This not only helps the species for its own growth but also helps other species surrounding it to grow and solve some of their problems. The overall development of the biosphere makes the planet more liveable and beautiful.

11. The Zigons

No power in this universe has the right to destroy another thriving civilization in this universe, how small or irrelevant it is. Different civilizations can thrive together a civilization destroyed by another should not be taken for granted and should be fought fiercely by one and all. Any threat, however great can be fought over in the united formation.

www.ingramcontent.com/pod-product-compliance
Lightning Source LLC
LaVergne TN
LVHW100338181026
850499LV00039B/1128

* 9 7 8 9 3 5 4 5 8 3 7 5 9 *